Disney

MINNIE MOUSE

D0730379

BIG DREAMS

A GRAPHIC NOVEL

by Brooke Vitale

graphix

An Imprint of

SCHOLASTIC

© 2021 Disney Enterprises, Inc. All rights reserved.

All rights reserved. Published by Graphix, an imprint of Scholastic Inc., *Publishers since 1920.* SCHOLASTIC, GRAPHIX, and associated logos are trademarks and/or registered trademarks of Scholastic Inc.

The publisher does not have any control over and does not assume any responsibility for author or third-party websites or their content.

No part of this publication may be reproduced, stored in a retrieval system, or transmitted in any form or by any means, electronic, mechanical, photocopying, recording, or otherwise, without written permission of the publisher. For information regarding permission, write to Scholastic Inc., Attention: Permissions Department, 557 Broadway, New York, NY 10012.

This book is a work of fiction. Names, characters, places, and incidents are either the product of the author's imagination or are used fictitiously, and any resemblance to actual persons, living or dead, business establishments, events, or locales is entirely coincidental.

ISBN 978-1-338-74329-6

10 9 8 7 6 5 4 3 2 1 21 22 23 24 25

Printed in the U.S.A. 40

First edition, September 2021
Written by Brooke Vitale
Illustrated by Artful Doodlers, Ltd.
Book design by Jeff Shake

PART 1

FIRST DAY OF SCHOOL

GULP.
1st Day of School

SCHOOL
YOU CAN DO IT, MINNIE.
YOU CAN HAVE THE BEST FIRST DAY OF SCHOOL EVER.
DON'T THINK ABOUT SCARY THINGS LIKE . . .

WHAT IF I GET LOST?

WHAT IF I GET LOST IN SPACE?

WHAT IF I GET LOST IN A JUNGLE?
HISSS

RAW!!
NERP!!
WHAT IF I GET LOST AND THE OTHER KIDS ARE MONSTERS?!

PLEASE DON'T LET THERE BE MONSTERS.

RING
RING
RING

HELLO?

EXCUSE ME . . .
COULD ANYONE . . . ?

LOOKS LIKE I HAVE TO HANDLE THIS MYSELF. THAT'S **OKAY**! I'M MINNIE. I CAN HANDLE ANYTHING . . . HOPEFULLY.

BANG!
BANG!
WHAT WAS THAT?
THE DOOR!

1st Day of School
THUD
RRRR...
DRAGON!

YOU CAN DO THIS, MINNIE.
IT'S JUST A DRAGON.
CHARGE!

SWISH!
TAKE THAT, YOU DRAGON!!!

DRAGON . . . MOP. HUH. AT LEAST IT WASN'T A MONSTER!
NOW, WHERE'S MY CLASSROOM?

OR SOMEONE I CAN ASK?
IT'S JUST YOUR IMAGINATION, MINNIE. THAT'S NOT A DRAGON. IT CAN'T BE A DRAGON.

AAAAH RUN!
AAAAH! RUN!

OH! YOU'RE NOT A DINOSAUR!
OH! YOU'RE NOT A DRAGON!
A DINOSAUR?
WHY WOULD I BE A DINOSAUR?
UNLESS . . . THIS KID IS LOST LIKE ME!

DAISY
HI. I'M DAISY.

Minnie Minnie
I'M MINNIE.
DID WE JUST BECOME FRIENDS?

BEST
FRIENDS!

TWO LOST BEST FRIENDS.

!
I HAVE AN IDEA!

WE NEED TO CALL FOR HELP.

HOW?
WELL, SINCE WE DON'T SEE ANY ADULTS . . . MAYBE THEY CAN HEAR US!
AND WE'LL GET TO USE MICROPHONES!

AUDIO
ROOM

THIS MUST BE IT!
CHARGE!

ARE WE SURE THIS IS A GOOD IDEA?
WE'RE SURE IT MIGHT BE A GOOD IDEA!

DO YOU THINK THIS WORKS?
ONLY ONE WAY TO FIND OUT!

BAD NEWS.
THIS DOOR DOESN'T OPEN FROM THE INSIDE.
IT'S TOO RUSTY.
WE'RE STUCK!
HELLO?
CAN ANYONE HEAR ME?
I DON'T THINK THIS THING IS ON.

HMM.
WHAT WOULD ONE OF MY FAVORITE CHARACTERS DO?
THEY'D MAKE A SIGN!

Help!
We're lost

ANY MOMENT SOMEONE WILL FIND US.
ANY.
MOMENT.
NOW.
Help!
We're lost

SIGH.

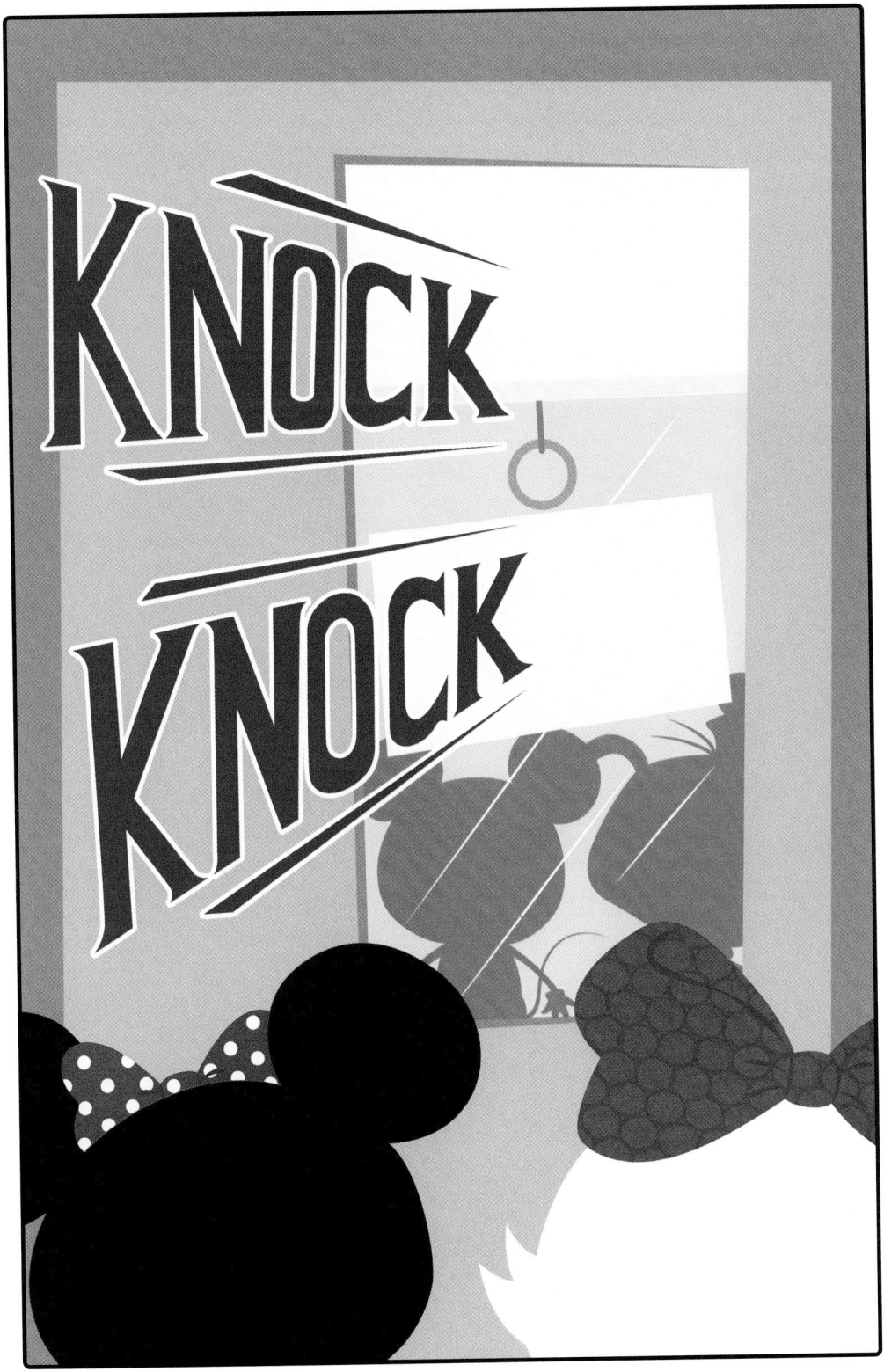
KNOCK
KNOCK

SOMEONE'S HERE.
PLEASE COME IN!
WE'RE LOST!
JUST DON'T CLOSE—
THE DOOR.
SLAM!

HOO HOO!
I'M GOOFY.
I'M MICKEY.
AND YOU TWO ARE LOST?
HALL MONITOR
I'M MINNIE.
THE DOOR WON'T OPEN.
I'M AFRAID YOU'RE STUCK HERE WITH US NOW, TOO.
I'M DAISY.

GAWRSH, THAT'S OKAY!
I'LL SIGNAL ANOTHER HALL MONITOR.
HALL MONITOR
BEEP!

KNOCK
KNOCK
SOMEONE'S COMING!

OH, THANK YOU, MR. HALL MONITOR, SIR!
BUT PLEASE DON'T CLOSE THE—
CLICK!
DOOR.
IT LOOKS LIKE YOU'RE HERE WITH US, TOO.

OH, NO.
WHAT IF WE'RE STUCK IN HERE FOR . . . EVER?

WE TRIED TO MAKE AN ANNOUNCEMENT, BUT NO ONE HEARD US.

C'MON, MINNIE, THINK!
YOU CAN DO THIS.
I KNOW YOU CAN!

HOLD ON.
I THINK WE NEED TO PLUG THE MICROPHONE IN!
WE CAN TRY THIS AGAIN!
WE MIGHT BE RESCUED!

PFFZZ

MINNIE, YOU DID IT!
MINNIE TO THE RESCUE!
GAWRSH.
MINNIE IS A HERO!
SHE DID IT!

HELLO?
MY NAME IS MINNIE, AND I'M IN THE AUDIO ROOM WITH MY FRIEND DAISY AND THREE OF THE SCHOOL'S VERY BEST, HIGHLY ESTEEMED—
I WOULDN'T GO THAT FAR.
AMAZING HALL MONITORS, AND WE NEED HELP!

WE'VE BEEN LOOKING EVERYWHERE FOR YOU KIDS!
NO WONDER WE COULDN'T FIND YOU.
THIS ROOM IS SO SMALL.
COME ALONG, NOW.
WE DID IT!

PART 2

RECESS TIME!

YOU CAN DO THIS.
EVEN IF YOU WEREN'T VERY GOOD AT SPORTS AT YOUR OLD SCHOOL,
THIS IS YOUR CHANCE TO GET THE BALL GAME RIGHT.

OR NOT.

IT'S OKAY, MINNIE.
IT'S JUST ONE STRIKE.
COME ON, MINNIE!
YOU CAN DO IT!

IMAGINE THIS IS A VIDEO GAME.
LEVEL 1

ONE, TWO, THREE . . .

GAME
OVER

OUCH!

JUST KICK.

BUT WHAT IF I'M THE REASON WE LOSE?
WILL DAISY STILL BE MY FRIEND?

WILL ANYONE BE MY FRIEND?

NO!
THEY'RE MY FRIENDS, WIN OR LOSE.
AND I'M MINNIE.
I AM GOING TO . . .

...WIN!

YEAH, MINNIE!
RUN!

OUT!
HUH?
WHAT HAPPENED?

PETE TAGGED YOU OUT.
DIDN'T YOU FEEL IT?
AH, PHOOEY!

SO,
WE LOST?

I'M SORRY.
I RUINED EVERYTHING.

RUINED?
THAT KICK WAS AMAZING! YOU DID GREAT!
I DID?

OF COURSE YOU DID!
PETE WAS JUST FASTER THAN YOU.
SO, YOU'RE NOT MAD?

I'LL ONLY BE MAD IF YOU KEEP THOSE KICKING SECRETS TO YOURSELF.

I LEARNED HOW TO KICK AT MY OLD SCHOOL.
WE USED TO BUILD GIANT OBSTACLE COURSES.
IT WAS A TRADITION TO KICK A BALL DURING THE COURSE.

HMM.
I'VE NEVER DONE AN OBSTACLE COURSE BEFORE.
REALLY?
IT'S TIME TO CHANGE THAT!

DAISY'S VERY FIRST OBSTACLE COURSE EVER. LIKE, EVER.

OBSTACLE COURSES ARE REALLY FUN.
YOU HAVE TO JUMP HIGH TO WIN—AND KICK LOTS TO GET INTO POSITION!
I'M IN!
DAISY'S VERY FIRST OBSTACLE COURSE EVER. LIKE, EVER.

OKAY, YOU WANT TO NOT THINK SO MUCH, AND LIFT YOUR FOOT, AND—

WAS THAT PETE? THAT WASN'T NICE.
HA, HA!

IGNORE HIM.
HE'S A MEANIE.
NOW, KICK!

UGH.
I CAN'T GET
NYTHING RIGHT.

YOU CAN DO THIS, DAISY.
PROMISE?
PROMISE!

I'M SORRY, MINNIE.
I JUST CAN'T STOP THINKING ABOUT HOW PETE IS SO MEAN.

YOU KNOW PETE'S HAT?
ETEND THE BALL S PETE'S HAT!
NOW, KICK!

OKAY.
KICKING!
HIGH SCORE
1UP

YOU DID IT, DAISY!
NOW JUMP TO FINISH THE COURSE!
DAISY'S VERY FIRST OBSTACLE COURSE EVER. LIKE, EVER.

VERY FIRST
STACLE COURSE
R LIK
THANKS, MINNIE.
SCHOOL SURE IS GOING TO BE BETTER WITH YOU AROUND!